KU-616-235

THE ADVENTURES OF ODYSSEUS

retold by
HUGH LUPTON
AND
DANIEL MORDEN

illustrated by
CHRISTINA BALIT

Barefoot Books
step inside a story

·CONTENTS·

·PROLOGUE·

One bright morning Prince Paris was out hunting. He was climbing the high rocky slopes of Mount Ida. Far below him his father's walled city, the city of Troy, lay like a circlet of stone, a shining diadem of towers. As he climbed, there was a sudden shimmer of light to one side of the stony mountain path.

Paris turned and saw Hermes, the messenger of the Gods. He knew him at once by his winged sandals. Hermes smiled his inscrutable, playful smile. 'Paris,' he said. 'I have been sent by great father Zeus, the Cloud-compeller. He has told me to tell you that you must decide which of these three Goddesses is the most beautiful.'

Hermes clicked his fingers and Paris was blinded by light. He covered his face with his hands. Slowly he opened his fingers and saw standing before him the three most powerful Goddesses of all.

There was Hera, the wife of Zeus, the Queen of Heaven, terrifying in her brilliance. There was owl-eyed Athene, the fierce and implacable Goddess of War and Wisdom. And there was beautiful Aphrodite, the Goddess of Love, to whose lilting tune the whole world dances.

Hermes gestured to the Goddesses with his hand. 'Paris, when you have decided which of these three is the most beautiful, you must give her this golden apple.'

Suddenly Paris felt the cold weight of a golden apple against the palm of his hand. He looked down at it. When he looked up again, Hermes was gone. The three Goddesses glowered at him. Paris's mouth went dry. He knew that if he chose one, the others would hate him. And the hatred of a Goddess is something to be avoided at all costs.

He stood motionless, dumbfounded, hardly daring to breathe. Hera, the magnificent Queen of Heaven, stepped forward. She whispered urgently, 'Paris, choose me and I will give you power. Choose me and I will make you a great king — half the world will be yours.' She stepped back.

Athene came forward, her grey eyes shining with light. 'Paris, choose me and you'll never lose a battle. Choose me and you will be famous the length and breadth of the world for your wisdom.'

She stepped back.

It was Aphrodite's turn. The Goddess of Love stepped towards Paris, smelling of musk and honey. Her voice was deep and enchanting. 'Paris, choose me, and I will give you the most beautiful woman in the world.'

'Who is she?' whispered Paris.

'Her name is Helen. She is the wife of red-haired Menelaus, the king of Sparta. I will blind her with love for you. She will give you everything!'

'What does she look like?'

Aphrodite smiled. 'She is as beautiful as I am.'

Then she stepped back.

Paris lifted the golden apple above his shoulder. The choice was clear as daylight.

'The golden apple goes to Aphrodite.'

Aphrodite was true to her word. She made Helen fall in love with Paris. Paris stole her from her husband and carried her across the blue Aegean Sea to the city of Troy. Menelaus was beside himself with rage. He sent messengers to all the other Greek kings — Agamemnon, Nestor, Ajax, Odysseus — and a huge army set sail. For ten long years they laid siege to Troy.

Hera and Athene, furious that they hadn't been given the golden apple, threw in their lot with the Greeks. And those vengeful Goddesses didn't rest until Troy's walls were crumbling, blood-soaked rubble and Paris was dead.

When the city had been destroyed, when Menelaus had won back his wife, the Greek kings set sail for home, swollen with pride, their ships crammed with the spoils of war.

1 ·THE STRANGER·

Nine long years had passed since that great and terrible victory. Nine summers and nine winters had passed, and on the island of Ithaca the people were still waiting for the return of their king, for Odysseus had not come home from the Trojan War. Every day his wife Penelope looked out over the restless sea wondering whether he was dead or alive. Every day his son Telemachus — who had been a baby when the war began and was now nineteen years old — wondered whether his father's body was rolling somewhere deep beneath the blue waves.

The island was in a state of chaos. It had been without a king for nineteen years. Suitors had invaded Odysseus's feasting hall, a motley company of princes, warriors, merchants and chancers trying their luck. All of them were hoping to win Penelope's hand in marriage, and trying to persuade her that Odysseus was dead. But Penelope refused to believe them. She clung to the slender hope that somewhere in the wide world he was still alive. She had told the suitors that she would only choose a new husband when

she had finished weaving a shroud for Odysseus's father. Every day she sat working at the loom. But every night, by the light of the moon, she unravelled all that she had woven during the day, so the shroud was never finished. And the suitors waited, passing the time by drinking Odysseus's wine, slaughtering his cattle, flirting with his maidservants and mocking his memory.

Meanwhile, on another island, a stranger was staggering out of the sea. His hair and beard were tangled and matted with salt. His whole body was caked with brine. Half dead with exhaustion, he crawled on his hands and knees across the sand. He made his way to a grove of trees and buried himself beneath the leaves scattered on the ground.

He closed his eyes and fell instantly into the sweet, oblivious balm of sleep.

It was the daughter of the king of that island who found him. Her name was Nausicaa. At first she thought the stranger was dead. But when she cautiously reached down and touched his arm, it was warm. She shook his shoulder and woke him. She fetched him a cup of water

and a piece of cloth to cover his nakedness. She led the stranger to her father's palace. She showed him a room where he could wash himself and she sent servants to bring him clothes.

As soon as he was alone, the stranger sponged himself from head to foot, washing the salt from his skin. He rubbed oil into his shoulders, neck and arms. He dressed himself in the fine clothes. Then Princess Nausicaa led him to her father's bronze-floored feasting hall.

King Alcinous was sitting on his throne. He looked the stranger up and down. 'Sit down. Eat! Drink!' he said.

Meat, bread, wine, honey-cakes, barley-meal and water were served. Gratefully the stranger sat at a table and ate. He ate for a long time. When at last his raging appetite had been satisfied and he was sitting back in his chair and wiping the crumbs from the corners of his mouth, King Alcinous said, 'There is food for the body, and there is food for the soul. Stranger, now that you have eaten, sit back and listen. My storyteller will entertain and enrich you with a story.'

The doors of the hall were thrown open and an old, blind storyteller was led into the hall. He stared in front of him as though he was peering into a world nobody else could see, his eyes yellowy-white and swollen with cataracts. He lifted his lyre to his shoulder and started to play. He threw back his head and burst into song:

I sing of the bronze Scaean gates of the city of Troy.
I sing of those bronze gates swinging open
And the mighty Trojan army riding out
With a whirring of wheels and a creaking of chariots,
With a neighing of horses and a shouting of men,
With a thundering of hooves and marching feet.
I sing of Prince Paris, his cloak billowing behind him,
His sword hungry for the savour of blood.
I sing of the Trojan army pouring across the plain.
And I sing of the clash of bronze against bronze
As the Trojan army meets the Greeks,
Like two rivers in full spate,
Each with its flotsam of uprooted trees,
Crashing into one another.

And I sing of the Greek heroes;
Mighty Achilles severing heads with every stroke,
Nimble-witted Odysseus trailing a wake of the dead
And old Nestor fierce among his foes . . .

'STOP!' King Alcinous put his hand on the old man's shoulder. 'Stop! Stop! Our guest — he is weeping. His face is buried in his hands. His shoulders are shaking. Stranger, who are you? Why does this story bring such grief?'

The stranger lifted his head and looked at the king, his cheeks wet and glistening with tears.

King Alcinous got up from his throne and seized one of the stranger's hands.

'Nobody, whether of high or low degree, goes nameless in this world. Tell us who you are. We will listen to your story and learn. And I will send one of my high-prowed ships to take you to the place you are seeking.'

The stranger looked into the king's face. He looked at the old storyteller and the princess. Then he slowly drew himself up to his full height, took a deep breath, and began to speak:

I have used many names, but the name by which you would know me is Odysseus. To hear this story fills me with emotion. It fills my eyes with tears to hear the name of my friend Achilles, whose bones now lie under Trojan sand. But to hear myself described as a hero, a man of honour, makes me want to laugh.

I remember the day when I first heard that red-haired Menelaus, King of Sparta, was mustering an army to fight against Troy. It was the

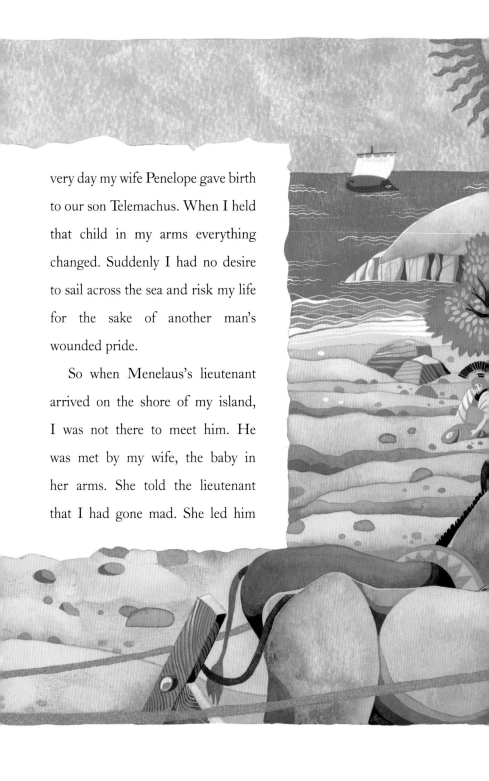

very day my wife Penelope gave birth to our son Telemachus. When I held that child in my arms everything changed. Suddenly I had no desire to sail across the sea and risk my life for the sake of another man's wounded pride.

So when Menelaus's lieutenant arrived on the shore of my island, I was not there to meet him. He was met by my wife, the baby in her arms. She told the lieutenant that I had gone mad. She led him to a beach where he found me, my face streaked with dirt, my hair in greasy ringlets, and my clothes no more than filthy rags. I had harnessed a donkey and an ox to a plough. I was ploughing the shingle, sowing handfuls of salt over my shoulder into the furrows that I had made, raving all the while.

This lieutenant was suspicious. Already I was famous for my cunning. Before I understood what he was doing, he had grabbed the baby, run forward and put it down in front of the plough. When I saw what he had done, I knew he had outwitted me. If I were to continue my pretence of madness I would have to cut the baby in half with the blade of the plough. I had to admit that I was sane. I mustered an army from among my subjects and I joined the great host that laid siege to the walls of Troy.

All of us went a little mad during the war, what with the betrayals and the intrigues, the interventions of the immortals and the stupid petty arguments amongst ourselves. My ship was crammed with precious things when I set sail for home. As we voyaged, in my mind's eye I could see the hero's welcome I would receive when at last I reached rocky

Ithaca. I could almost see the streets of my land, lined with my people cheering. I could see myself stepping over the threshold of my feasting hall to find my beloved wife. My son would be a ten-year-old boy now. I could see the pride in the eyes of my father. I could almost feel my mother's warm embrace.

2 ·THE·CYCLOPS·

For many days we sailed until we reached an island that seemed to us a paradise. We saw land, level for the plough, fat sheep and goats grazing.

We decided to stop and take on fresh meat and water. We beached the ship. I told twelve of my men to take from the treasures of Troy some precious thing, some bracelet or brooch, in the hope that we would find people with whom we could barter. I took a goatskin of a strong wine. One cupful poured into a barrel of water would still make a potent potion.

We followed a path from the beach to a hill. In the hill there was a cave. Beside the cave there was a boulder that looked as though it had been placed there for some purpose. Perhaps this cave was a home. Sure enough, when we went inside we found enclosures with fences which held lambs and kids. We found buckets of cheese and milk. Whose home was this? We squatted by a fire, munched some cheese, drank some milk, sat back and waited.

Eventually we heard bleating. A great flock of animals was approaching. Something — perhaps a premonition — made me instruct my men to hide in the darkest part of the cave. A huge herd of sheep and goats entered and gathered near their young.

Then, behind them, we saw a silhouette in the cave mouth. It was the shape of a man, but this was bigger than any man we had ever seen. It was the size of a tall tree. It lumbered in, grabbed the boulder and rolled it into the entrance. Now the only light came from the fire. By the light of the flames we watched the giant milk the female sheep and goats with surprising tenderness and obvious affection. We studied its tusk-like teeth and its snout of a nose. In the middle of its forehead there was one enormous eye.

By the light of the fire he must have seen our shadows on the wall behind us. He said, 'What's this? I have guests! Little two-eyed things!'

We stepped forward. 'We are men. We have here precious treasures. We want to swap them with you for meat

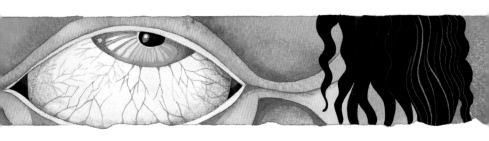

and fresh water. Father God Zeus rewards those who are kind to travellers.'

'Zeus? Don't you know what I am? I am a Cyclops. We Cyclopes are the sons of the Sea God Poseidon. We have no fear of your blustering Zeus!'

Then the Cyclops grabbed one of my men and smacked his head against the roof of the cave. His brains splattered against the walls and the floor. He crammed the corpse into his mouth.

We were horrified. Before he could devour another of my men I held up the skin of strong wine. 'We little two-eyes have made something you one-eyes have not. It is drink that makes you happy. If I give it to you, would you give me a gift in return?'

'Give me your gift, and I will give you an answer!'

I threw the wineskin to his feet. He picked it up, took the stopper from it and emptied it in one long gulp. He threw it to the ground.

'What is your name?' he asked.

23

'My name? My name is Nobody.'

'Well, then, Nobody, I thank you for your gift. It tasted good. In return I will give something precious: a little more life. I promise you will be the last one that I eat!'

He grabbed another one of my men and bit off his head. As the Cyclops chewed his cheeks reddened. His great eyelids met. He put out his hand to steady himself. The wine was taking effect. Soon he lay on the ground, his cheek against the sand, his eye shut, his mouth open, dripping blood and wine.

One of my crew drew his sword and stepped forward, intending to plunge the blade through the Cyclops's skin and kill him as he slept. I had to restrain him. The Cyclops was our only means of escape. All of us together weren't strong enough to push the rock from the cave mouth. We were trapped until this brute freed us.

All that night we searched the cave. We found the trunk of an olive tree that the Cyclops was drying to use as a

shepherd's crook. We drew our swords and whittled at it until it came to a sharp point. We put the point into the fire, until it glowed red-hot. We lifted the tree trunk on to our shoulders, and, urging each other on, we ran forwards and plunged the point into his eye, twisting it from side to side as we did so. Steam rose up around the wood. The Cyclops gave an awful yell. He reared up and pulled the wood from his head with a sucking sound. The scream summoned other Cyclopes from nearby caves. We could hear them shouting through the boulder, 'Polyphemus, what's the matter?'

'I have been blinded!'

'Who has blinded you?'

'Nobody! Nobody has blinded me!'

'If nobody has blinded you, there's nothing we can do to help you. It must be a punishment from the immortals! Pray to them and your sight will be restored to you!' And so the other Cyclopes went back to their caves and their slumbers.

All that night we played a terrible game of blind man's buff with Polyphemus.

He felt his way around the walls of the cave, uttering threats and insults, the blood dripping from his chin. We ducked under his swooping hands. Eventually, when the animals' bleating alerted the Cyclops to the coming of the day, he felt his way along the walls of the cave until he touched the boulder that blocked the cave mouth. He pushed it out.

He turned and squatted in the entrance, his back protruding out of the cave and his legs apart. He felt across the floor until he found the fences. He opened them and the flock made its way out to graze. Of course, they had to pass through his legs and under him. As they did so he ran his fingers over their backs. Polyphemus was hoping we would try to escape by hiding among them. He was hoping he would recognise us by our human shape and pull us limb from limb. But I had guessed he would do this.

During the night my companions and I had tied the sheep together, in rows of three, one beside the other. Then each of my men had slid under the belly of the middle sheep, and I had tied him beneath the animal. When the Cyclops ran his hands over the sheep, all he felt was the wool of their backs. In this way my men escaped. Only I remained. I had held back a great curly-horned ram. Now I slid under its belly, reached up and grabbed the wool on its neck. I shook it. The ram trotted towards Polyphemus. He touched its horns.

His fingers closed around the ram's head. The ram stopped. The Cyclops said, 'I know you. You are the chief of the herd. Every morning you are the first to leave the cave. And yet today, when all the others have gone, you linger. Why?'

Under the ram I was sure that my heart was beating so loudly that the Cyclops would hear it. Then I heard him say, 'I know why. Somehow you know that I am suffering, don't you? You want to stay with me, and console me with your company. But there is nothing you can do. I am blind now. You must go and graze with your companions.'

He released the beast. It trotted out into the daylight. I was free! I untied my men and we herded the sheep down to the ship. We made the water white with the blades of

our oars. I looked back at this island that so recently had seemed to us a paradise. I could see the hill and the cave. I could see the Cyclops in the cave entrance. He was still waiting for us to make our move. And I couldn't stop myself. I had to gloat.

'Polyphemus! It was not Nobody who blinded you! It was somebody! It was Odysseus! A ram among sheep! King of rocky Ithaca! Remember my name for the rest of your life of stumbling darkness!'

'Father Poseidon! Did you hear his name? It was Odysseus who blinded your son. Blight his voyage with trial and calamity, so that if at last he reaches his homeland, let it be alone, and unknown, and under a strange sail, and let him find danger waiting where there should be a welcome!'

I laughed at the Cyclops's ranting, but my gloating would cost us dearly . . .

3 ·THE·SACK·OF·WINDS·

The ocean was calm. There was not a breath of a breeze on the sea. My men had to row until their hands were studded with blisters. They bandaged their hands. The blood oozed through the bandages. Day after day they toiled. It was as if we were crossing the surface of a mirror.

At last we saw that something was approaching us. It was flashing and bobbing, reflecting the light of the sun. A floating island, surrounded by walls of bronze! I'd heard stories of this place from sailors. I'd heard it offered a welcome, and sure enough when we came closer the guards atop those bronze walls shouted, 'King Aeolus offers sanctuary in exchange for tales of your adventures!'

We rowed through a pair of bronze gates and tethered our ship to the jetty. We were led up a cobblestone hill to the bronze palace of the mad king Aeolus. He loved to hear the stories of the world, but he would never choose to leave his island. For seven days and nights his hall echoed with our tales. We filled our bellies with roasted meat.

All this time, there was not the faintest whisper of wind outside. When I mentioned this to Aeolus, he cackled and nodded his head.

At last, the time had come to resume our voyage. His soldiers led my men down to the harbour. The old king gestured to me to follow him up a flight of stairs to his bedroom. He led me to a curtain in the corner. Gleefully he pulled it back. I saw an alcove. I saw a sack tied tight with a silver thong. It writhed and wriggled. The king looked carefully around. Then he gestured to me to come closer. I came so close I could taste his breath on my tongue.

He whispered, 'Zeus is my friend. He's in the middle of a feud with his brother Poseidon. He has stolen the winds of the world from the Sea God and put them in this sack! He has given it to me for safe keeping. I am to open it when I see fit. It crosses my mind that I could let out one gust to fill your sail. With that wind behind you, you'd be carried across the surface of the sea as surely as an arrow loosed from a bow. I will give the sack to you. When at last you

plant your feet on Ithacan shingle you can open it and set free the gusts and gales. You will soon be home!'

I wept for joy. The old man knelt beside the sack and untied the knot in the silver thong. He dipped his hand inside and pulled out what appeared to me to be a writhing snake of smoke. He opened his hand and the snake vanished. We shivered. Aeolus pulled the thong tight again and gave the sack to me.

The king and I went down the cobblestone hill to the harbour. I climbed aboard the ship. I placed the sack just behind the prow, on the foredeck. My men were waiting at their benches. The people of the island were lining the jetty. I shouted, 'King Aeolus has given me the finest gift that ever I received in my entire life. This sack holds a treasure greater than all the spoils of Troy!'

His subjects cheered, and the king beamed from ear to ear. My crew stared at the sack.

Once we were out of those bronze gates we unfurled the sail and lifted the oars from the water. The old man spoke

the truth! The sail filled with wind.
No need to row, no need to steer! It
was as if we were following a path
across the trackless waves of the sea.

For nine days and nights I sat on
the foredeck, the sack by my side. I
kept a vigil, scanning the horizon,
never sleeping, desperate for a
glimpse of Ithaca. Then there she
was. I knew her shape so well — the
valleys, the secret places only I had
seen, the terraces, the vineyards, the
beaches — the outline of my beloved
Ithaca! Great Mount Neriton rising

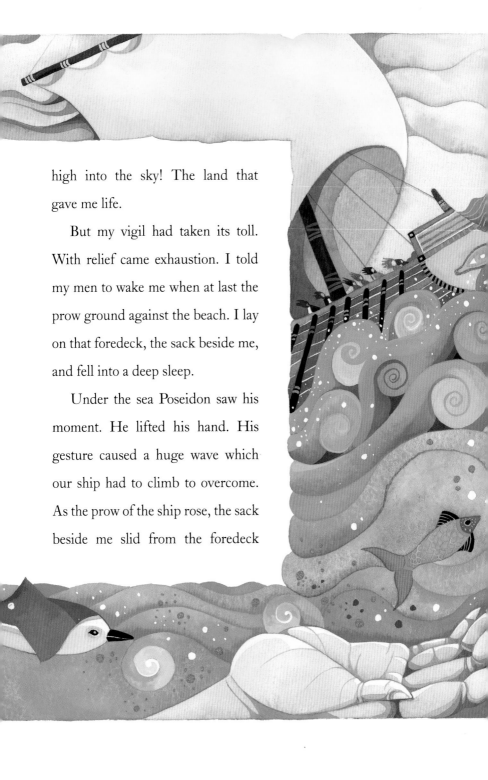

high into the sky! The land that gave me life.

But my vigil had taken its toll. With relief came exhaustion. I told my men to wake me when at last the prow ground against the beach. I lay on that foredeck, the sack beside me, and fell into a deep sleep.

Under the sea Poseidon saw his moment. He lifted his hand. His gesture caused a huge wave which our ship had to climb to overcome. As the prow of the ship rose, the sack beside me slid from the foredeck and landed in the lap of one of my crew. He turned to one of his friends and said, 'Did you hear what Odysseus told that king? He said this sack contained the finest gift he had ever he received. Everything else he's shared with us. He ought to share this, too. After all, we've risked our lives as often as he has. But this treasure he seems to want to keep for himself. Where's the justice in that? What harm would there be in seeing what he has been given?'

He untied the silver thong. He pushed his thumbs into the mouth of the sack and as he did so he was blasted from his bench on to the deck! He saw a thousand wriggling snakes of smoke rising from the sack into the sky!

Poseidon had all the weapons he needed now. The sky darkened. The waves rose up around us. The sail was torn to shreds. The ship was spinning. The spinning woke me. I sat up. Poseidon spat brine into my eyes. I looked for Ithaca but already she was so vague that she might have been just the edge of a cloud.

I reached out across the side of the ship and tried to clutch at her, as if to pull her towards me but she was gone. I was so seized with despair it was all I could do to hold back from hurling myself into the waves. The north wind tossed us for the south wind to catch. The west and the east winds fought over us. Sometimes we were climbing mountains of water. Sometimes we were sinking into valleys and the sky could not be seen. It was clear that Poseidon wanted us dead. How would we ever see our homes, our hearths, our fields and farms and families again?

4 ·CIRCE·

As soon as we sighted land we made for it. We beached the ship and dragged it up out of the reach of even the fiercest wave. Once the ship was safe, the storm abated. It was plain that this tempest had been sent by Poseidon.

My men sank into dark despair. They sat on the shore and wept but I am always craning my neck towards the horizon, yearning for the place where the sea meets the sky. I decided I would explore this place that our bitter fate had brought us to.

I climbed a hill to survey the island. Not far from where we'd landed there was a forest. In the forest there was a clearing. I saw in the clearing a white palace of a strange design. This island was inhabited! Perhaps these people could provide us with some way to placate or outwit the Sea God.

I ran back to the ship to tell my men what I had seen, but it was deserted. I found their footprints leading into the forest. I followed them into the clearing I had seen from the hill, but between the palace and me there was a pack of lions and wolves.

I drew my sword and crept towards the first of them. It was a lion. As I approached it, it closed its eyes, flattened its ears and purred! I could stroke the velvet fur between its eyes. It licked my hand. Next I approached a wolf. It rolled on to its back and showed me its belly to scratch. What kind of wild beasts were these?

When I reached the palace I looked through the window. I could see my crew. They were sitting round a table laughing and singing, eating and drinking as if they were home.

Out of the shadows behind them came the mistress of this place. Long-limbed she was, pale-skinned, dark-haired and dark-eyed. She brought them cheese and wine and honey and barley-meal. As they ate I saw her take a wand from beneath her skirts. She touched each of them in turn. As each man was touched he dropped the cup he had been clutching and stared at his fingers as they grew together. His arms and legs shrank to stubs. His belly swelled and his nose stretched out into a snout. These were no longer men — for sitting around the table I could see only pigs!

The lady clapped her hands, and the pigs flopped from their stools and followed her into the shadows. Now I understood. The lions and wolves had once been human. She had tested them, and had found them wanting.

Half of me was furious. The other half was terrified.

I drew my sword, intending to rush in and attack, but then all the hairs on the back of my neck stood up.

I knew this sensation. I knew this meant I was in the presence of a God or Goddess. Sure enough, shimmering above me was the messenger of the Gods,

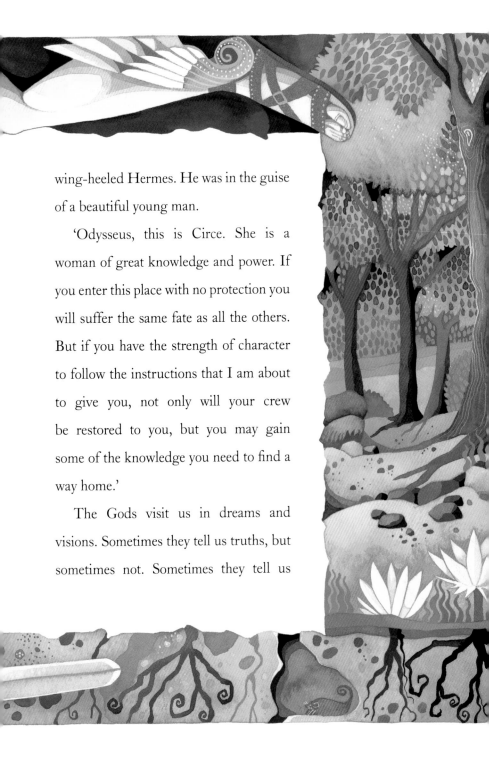

wing-heeled Hermes. He was in the guise of a beautiful young man.

'Odysseus, this is Circe. She is a woman of great knowledge and power. If you enter this place with no protection you will suffer the same fate as all the others. But if you have the strength of character to follow the instructions that I am about to give you, not only will your crew be restored to you, but you may gain some of the knowledge you need to find a way home.'

The Gods visit us in dreams and visions. Sometimes they tell us truths, but sometimes not. Sometimes they tell us

half-truths, to betray us. I saw it happen at Troy. Hermes is not just the Messenger of the Gods; he is also the God of Trickery and Storytelling. But what choice did I have? I could not sail my ship alone.

Hermes led me into the forest. He showed me a plant, black of root, white of petal. Moly is its name. This, he said, would protect me against Circe's enchantments. He picked it from the ground as only a God could do. He told me to pouch it within my cheek. I bowed my head to give thanks. When I lifted my head I was alone.

I was shaking as I approached Circe's palace. She opened the door and greeted me but I did not meet her eye. I knew if I looked into her eye for even a moment I would be enthralled by her. She led me to the table. I ate and drank, but all I tasted was the bitter root of Moly.

Suddenly I felt something cool touch my neck. Circe was standing over me with the wand in her hand. She gasped to see that her magic had had no effect.

I leaped to my feet. With my sword I struck the wand out of her hand. I showed her the sharp end of my blade

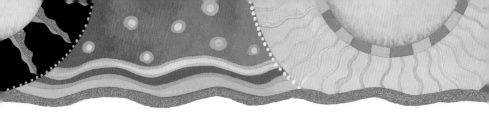

and said, 'You must promise there'll be no more tricks and restore my crew to their human form or you'll learn why they say my name means trouble.'

'Trouble!' she said. 'One hundred years ago there was a prophecy that a man would come who was worthy of the knowledge I bear. The prophecy said his name would mean trouble. You are Odysseus, Laertes's son, and you are welcome here. I promise I will only give you what you desire.'

She picked up the wand, and led me outside into the fierce sunlight. She walked to the pigsty and touched each beast in turn, and as she did so the pig once again became one of my crew, on his hands and knees, guzzling acorns. At first they were terrified of Circe, but when I told them of the promise she hadmade me, we returned to her palace. That night she gave us a great feast. Once my men were asleep she stroked my cheek and whispered, 'Odysseus, your ship is in need of repair. Your sail is torn to shreds. Don't go at once. Give me a little month before you sail away.'

'A month,' I said.

But one month became three, then six, and then nine.
After a year, the crew demanded that we leave. Reluctantly
I went to Circe and told her the time had come for us to
voyage on. I asked if she might know of a way to placate or
outwit the Sea God. She shook her head.

'I know who would have an answer to that question —
the blind prophet Tiresias,' she said.

'Where is he?' I said. 'I will consult him.'

Her answer put a chill into my soul. 'Tiresias lived and
died long ago. If you want to speak to him you must sail north
and north again until you reach the Land of the Dead.'

5 ·THE·LAND·OF·THE·DEAD·

Home is what a gull cries for over rough waters. There is nothing worse for mortal man than wandering. How many more storms before my ship could lower its sail?

I was haunted by memories of home. The long shadows of the afternoon stretching down the terraces and vineyards that ladder every slope, the scent of herbs on the breeze, the tongue of my dog against my palm, great Mount Neriton, the rocks, the goat tracks, the sandy beaches. A wife without a husband and a country without a king: these things compelled me to walk among the ghosts of the dead.

Circe gave us provisions and blankets. We soon discovered their purpose. The further north you sail, the colder it becomes. One morning when we woke, we could see our breath curling from our lips and our nostrils in a silver mist. A few days later we saw shards of ice hanging from the mast and the rigging. Then we found ourselves approaching a wall of fog that rose from the sea to the sky. I could not tell you for how long we sailed once we passed

inside that fog. Day and night had no meaning. There was only an endless clammy gloom.

The prow of the ship hit a sandbank. I and two of my companions took a pair of sheep ashore. We set off. The further we walked, the more uneasy we felt. Everything was infected with the greyness of the mist. All colour bled from our clothes and our skin. My companions became shifting forms in the fog beside me. My thoughts, too, became grey, sluggish, stupid, lumpen. Every doubt and regret I've ever felt crowded in on my mind, each with its own persuasive voice. All my old wounds ached. Every step took a little more effort. It was as if we were wading against the current of an ocean we couldn't see.

We reached the banks of a broad, oily river. It was the River of Forgetfulness. On the other side, hidden from our

view by the fog, was the Realm of Many Guests, the Land of the Dead.

We scooped a hole in the sand at our feet. We lifted the heads of the sheep and slit their throats. Their dark blood flowed into the hole. Shapes formed in the fog. We heard a moaning, a hissing. The ghosts of the dead were coming, summoned by our sacrifice. We saw young brides, warriors with gaping gashes, gurgling children. The sight of them made my soldiers shake with horror. Most of the spirits of the dead have lost all memory of their previous life. They are stupid, hungry wraiths until they can drink the blood of a mortal sacrifice. They long to remember their lives.

Our blood offering was for one of the few who has kept his mind: the blind prophet Tiresias. Though I had instructed my companions to hold back the flickering ghosts until

Tiresias had drunk his fill, they could do nothing but stand and shake and gape. It was as though they had fallen into some kind of trance. It was left to me to draw my sword and keep the dead at bay. One of the wraiths was as insubstantial as all the others, but he had a dignity, a purpose, that the others lacked. Surely this was Tiresias. I guided him with the sound of my voice towards the pool. He cupped his hands and drank. His white eyes twitched in their sockets.

'What can you see?'

'You are Odysseus. You seek a way back to rocky Ithaca, but it will be hard for you. Poseidon longs to avenge the mutilation of his son Polyphemus. There is only one way that you will see the lights of home again. You must learn humility. You must rein in your desires and those of your crew. During your voyage you will approach an island that will seem to you the perfect place to land. You'll see cattle grazing, no sign of human life. You will want to stop and feast on their flesh, but Odysseus, be warned, this herd is the prized possession of the Sun God Hyperion. If he were to see you harm them — and he is the Sun God, he sees all — he would go to Zeus and demand revenge. The Cyclops's curse would pursue you relentlessly. If ever you reached your homeland, it would be alone and unknown, and under a strange sail, and there would be danger waiting where there should be a welcome.

'If you can overcome this danger there is another journey you must make. You must put an oar on your shoulder and walk inland, leaving behind everyone, everything, everywhere you know. At last you will reach a crossroads. There a man will stop you and gaze in wonder at the oar. He will ask you what it is, whether it is some kind of winnowing fan for separating the grain.

'This is a place where they do not know what an oar is because they do not know what the sea is. This is a place where you truly are Nobody. In this place you must plant the blade of the oar in the ground so that the shaft rises up towards the sky. Make a sacrifice to great Poseidon of a ram, a bull and a breeding boar. Then you will have made your peace with him. If you can do all these things, your death will come to you in old age, from the sea, in the veils of sleep, like a long-awaited friend.

'This vision I have seen. It has come to me through a Gate of Horn.'

As the sightless seer spoke, more and more of the flickering ghosts gathered around the pool. I saw a sight then that struck me with such a shock of sorrow that I stumbled back and fell into the pool of blood. I turned and ran, screaming, my two companions following me, not knowing why they were running. Soon we were back on the ship and out on the open sea.

My companions never asked me what had put me to flight. I never told them that I had seen among the dead the face of my mother. I had been away so long that if I ever reached my homeland she would not be there. I would never again feel her warm embrace.

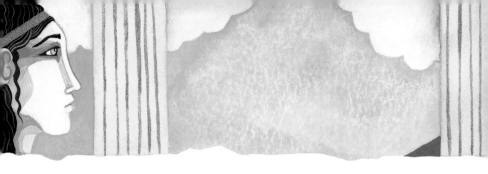

6 ·THE·SONG·OF·THE·SPHERES·

The smell of the dead clings to the nostrils. Only when we had passed out of the mist, when there was wind and tide, day and night, did we shake off the chill.

We returned to Circe's island. Once my men had eaten and were asleep, I told Circe what I had learned. She shook her head in wonder. 'Mortals are meant to have only one journey to that place. You alone will have two. Listen well to what I have to tell you. There are several trials you must undergo before you find the island of the Sun God Hyperion.'

Circe told me of the island of the Sirens, and their enchantments, and how I might evade them. She told me also of straits our ship would approach. 'The current will carry you into them. You cannot prevent it. To your left you will see rising sheer from the sea a column of rock, the sides

so smooth it is as if they have been polished, the summit
shrouded in thick smoke. In the column there is a cave. This
cave is the lair of an ancient, snake-necked, flame-skinned,
six-headed dragon. Her name is Scylla the Devourer. As
you pass through these straits she will lunge and eat six of
your crew. Better this than to sail too far to starboard.

'To your right you will see an island, broad and flat like
the back of a crab. One fig tree dips its branches into the
ocean beneath. Under the fig tree there is a whirlpool. Her
name is Charybdis, the Swallower. If your ship were to be
caught in the grip of her current not even great Zeus could
save you. This is why you must stay as close as you can to the
bottom of the dragon's tower.'

As soon as she had finished I asked, 'How can I kill
this Scylla?'

Circe shook her head. Then she pressed her fingers
against my lips.

'This is no place for acts of daring folly. There is a price, a toll, which must be paid for safe passage through these straits. Either you lose six lives or all of you die.'

The next morning, when dawn took her golden throne, we said our last farewells to Circe. She gave us a wind to fill our sail. When the wind failed us, when the sail sagged, we knew we were approaching the enchanted region of the Sirens.

The Sirens sing a song so beautiful that any mortal who hears it forgets everything except the desire to hear more. Many a ship has wrecked itself against the rocks that lurk beneath the sea around their island. But they are the daughters of a Muse. To pass so close to such beauty without experiencing it was unthinkable. I had to hear that song. I ordered my men to tie me to the mast and block their ears with wax. They were to ignore my instructions whilst I was under the Sirens' spell.

The shimmering song began. I begged my crew to change their course. I threatened them and cursed them but they were deaf to all my pleas. As they pulled at the oars they could see two white hills on the island.

When we were closer still they saw the hills were heaps of bones, bleached white by the sun. On top of each heap they could see a creature with the body of a vulture and the head of a woman, singing.

As for me I could see nothing. I could only hear a song so searingly beautiful I nearly lost all reason.

In the song I heard so many sounds: the beating of a swan's wings, the hiss and drag of the sea on shingle, the moan of the wind as it blows across the broad face of the world, the rhythm of the passage of the seasons, my wife singing — and all the sounds I heard were in harmony. For those few moments I heard the Song of the Spheres. Ever since then all music has been clatter to me; the sound of a shield as it falls on a cobblestone floor.

7 ·TORMENT·AND·TRIAL·

When the sail filled again we knew we were safe. My men untied me. I didn't have long to regain my composure. Soon a rock column rose above the horizon, the sides smooth, the summit shrouded in smoke. I walked between the benches with a brave word for each of my companions, then I stood before them and said, 'My friends, these straits we approach pose us a great danger, but surely no greater than the Cyclops, and we defeated him. Helmsman, steer a course towards the column of rock to port. There is a whirlpool to starboard. Oarsmen, your lives depend on the strength of your arms!'

I didn't tell them about the dragon who waited for us on top of that tower. If I had they would have hidden wherever they could, and I needed the strength of every man to break the whirlpool's grip.

Despite Circe's warnings, I put on my breastplate and a helmet, I took a spear in each hand and scanned the smoke hoping that I could fend Scylla off before she struck.

Then the air became clammy. The ship shook. The water around us was white, hissing and boiling. We saw the whirlpool. She was magnificent and beautiful, awful and terrible. She sucked down the ocean with such ferocity that we glimpsed the sea bed. Then she spat it into the sky so it fell on our cheeks like salty rain. We watched her, transfixed.

Then the dragon struck. Quick as thought, she lunged from her cave. Each of her six savage heads plucked one of my men from his bench. When they screamed I turned and

looked. For a moment I glimpsed her, her ancient mocking eyes, her fiery skin, the flailing limbs of one of my friends between her jaws. And then she was gone into the smoke.

I fought in a war for ten years. I saw men do awful things to other men. But I never saw a sight as terrible as that. They died screaming my name. The sound of their screams still haunts my dreams.

8 ·SHIPWRECKED·

Once we had escaped the dragon and the whirlpool we could do nothing. We sat at our benches and wept. The ship drifted where it would. Then one of my men sighted land. I saw cattle grazing, no sign of human life. I saw the sun staring down and I remembered the terrible prophecy of Tiresias. I told them we would voyage on. At this something snapped inside them. One of them, Eurylochus was his name, spat and stood.

'Odysseus,' he said. 'I am beginning to suspect you are not a man at all. I think you are one of the Gods in disguise. For like the Gods, you have no pity! We want to mourn the deaths of our friends! We want to recover from this awful ordeal but you insist we sail on blindly into the night, across a foreign sea when a friendly coast beckons us. I say we listen to our desires, not the ranting of a dead man!'

By the nodding of the heads around me, I saw it would be hard to cheat Poseidon of his quarry. I made them all solemnly promise me they wouldn't harm any of the cattle on the island. They did this at once. We still had plenty of the food from the gifts of Circe. And so we beached the ship, we lit a fire, we tried to eat, but none of us had any appetite. We were thinking of the victims of the dragon Scylla, our friends with whom we had seen so much. Many of us fell asleep with tears coursing down our cheeks.

I was woken during the third watch by Eurylochus shaking my shoulders. As soon as I opened my eyes I could see why. There was a terrible storm. It was as though the sea and the sky were at war with one another.

'You see!' shouted Eurylochus. 'If we'd listened to you, we'd have been out there now! By the morning our bones would have been rolling across the ocean bed.'

That storm howled throughout the night. It continued throughout the next day. It raged for a month. First we ran out of bread, then meat, then wine, then everything else we had. We were living on what we could find, what we could catch — birds' eggs, fish — and it was not enough. I began to understand the nature of the trap in which we were caught. I could see hunger gnawing at the patience and the bellies of my crew. They looked longingly at the cattle.

One morning I left them behind. I clambered over the dunes until I found a place where the ground was dry and there I lit a fire. I made what offerings I could. I prayed to the mighty immortals that they would end the storm so that we could sail away from this dangerous place. In return for my act of devotion, some God or Goddess kissed my eyelids and I fell into a deep sleep.

When I opened my eyes the sky was high and blue. I heard no moaning wind now, only birdsong. My clothes were dry. The storm had ended! I climbed over the dunes. There was the ship. Beside it my men were squatting round a fire. On the fire the carcasses of two of those cattle. Eurylochus saw me approaching. He pulled a lump of meat from one of the carcasses, held it up, and said, 'Odysseus, the Gods are not angry with us! We made offerings! We gave the best cuts of the meat to the Gods and Goddesses. As soon as we had done so the storm ended. They feel hunger too. All they expected was the respect they deserve! Eat!'

I looked at that meat and I saw a sight they could not see. The two carcasses on the fire opened their lipless mouths and moaned. That meat was cursed. Even though I was

starving I would not let it pass my lips. My men ate their fill and sealed their fates. They wrapped the hides around the remains of the meat. They loaded it aboard the ship. We unfurled a sail and lifted the oars.

As the island dipped beneath the horizon I shivered and looked around me. Suddenly the ship was in shadow. Blotting out the sun, there was the strangest cloud I had ever seen. It was as if blood was being dropped into clear water. It was swelling out and staining the sky. Then I heard Hyperion's cry for vengeance and Zeus answered it with a thunderbolt that struck our ship where the mast reached the deck. The mast crashed down and cracked open the head of my helmsman. The whole ship bucked. A wall of water rose against us. I could see into it, the brown weed quivering at the heart of it, and then it broke with a white roar and our ship was dashed to pieces. Fuming breakers tore at every plank. I sank beneath the surface. For a moment all was silent. I could feel the Sea God pressing against my eyelids, my nostrils, my lips, my ears.

Then I broke the surface and the world was filled with sound: the rumble of thunder, Poseidon's laughter, the crashing of the waves and the screams of my friends. I fought against the storm. Time and again I was sure the darkness would descend over my eyes. The surface of the ocean was white, hissing, boiling. The whirlpool! We were caught in the great grip of Charybdis. I kicked and fought, but she was far too strong for me.

A wave lifted me a little and I looked up. I saw something blacker than the night sky. I reached out and I clutched it. It was one of the branches of the fig tree that hung over Charybdis! As I hung from the tree I watched, shivering and moaning, as she dragged my men down, down, down until they were just black specks. She spat out their corpses and they bobbed lifeless in the brine. With a cry I let go of the branch. Taking advantage of the few moments between the suck and spout of the whirlpool, I hit the water near a piece of the ship and I grabbed it. I fought, I kicked and I prayed to the immortals on Mount Olympus that

I would pass out of these straits before the drag of the whirlpool began again.

Surely some God or Goddess was smiling on me. Somehow I made my way out of those straits before the whirlpool began to suck me down again. For many days and nights I clung to that piece of wood. More dead than alive, I was found on the shore of an island by a nymph. Her name was Calypso. She carried me to her cave where she nursed me back to health. As she nursed me she fell in love with me. She offered me immortal life if I would only stay with her. But as I lay there, unable to move, I knew that all I wanted from the rest of my life was a simple human thing.

I wanted to live, grow old and die with the woman I loved, my wife Penelope. And so I refused Calypso's offer.

She kept me on that island for seven years. Every day she tried to persuade me. For seven years I walked the shore of the island, staring out across the restless waves, longing for my homeland. For seven years I pondered all my moments of bravery and honour and arrogance and folly. Seven years to wonder that I had put my trust in the kindness of a witch and the vision of a blind man. I had become Nobody, and

I had heard the song nobody should hear. Seven years to wonder that I had refused the chance to live for ever for the sake of a woman I hadn't seen for half my life.

Eventually, prompted by the Goddess Athene, Calypso gave me the tools to build a raft. I lifted a mast, put a sail upon it, and once again I rode the broad, bucking back of Poseidon. By chance he saw me and raised a terrible storm, and my raft was destroyed. For three days I swam through the lashing, crashing waves.

Naked, I was found on the shores of this island, King Alcinous. Everything I took from Troy is gone — my treasure, my ship and my friends lie at the bottom of the sea. All I have left now is my name. And a longing as sharp as pain to see the land that gave me life.'

9 ·ITHACA·

Odysseus stood in the bronze-floored feasting hall of King Alcinous. He looked at the king, the princess and the old blind storyteller. There was a long silence broken at last by King Alcinous.

'Odysseus, you have suffered much in your wanderings across the broad face of the world, but now that you have reached my bronze-floored feasting hall I swear that I will send a high-prowed ship to carry you safely back home to rocky Ithaca. And I swear by the mighty Gods and Goddesses that you will not return to your homeland empty-handed.'

The king ordered that great chests of gold and silver, and rolls of purple cloth be fetched. They were carried down to the quayside, where a ship was waiting. They were loaded on to the deck of the ship. Odysseus was led down to the quayside. As he walked across the gangplank towards the deck he felt a hand tugging at his cloak. He turned and saw Princess Nausicaa.

'Odysseus,' she said. 'It is to me above all others that you owe your life. You will not forget me, will you?'

Odysseus smiled. 'Princess,' he said, 'if by the grace of the mighty Gods and Goddesses I set foot once again on the shores of my beloved Ithaca, I swear that I will remember you for as long as I draw breath.'

He stepped on to the deck and the sails were raised, the anchors were lifted, the wooden oars struck the waves and the prow cut a path through the churning waves. Soon the wind was filling the sails like a swollen belly. The ship made its way out of the harbour and across the blue sea.

Odysseus lay down on the deck and wrapped himself in his cloak. He closed his eyes and fell into the sweet oblivious balm of sleep. All that day he slept. The sun set and the sky darkened, and still he slept. The moon rose and set, the night brightened with countless stars, and still he was fast asleep.

He was still sleeping when the ship reached the island of Ithaca. The sailors lifted him tenderly in their arms and they waded ashore. They set him down gently on the shingle beach with the chests of treasure beside him. Then they returned to their ship and sailed away.

But nothing is hidden from the eyes of the mighty Gods and Goddesses. Owl-eyed Athene, the Goddess of War and Wisdom, was fond of Odysseus. He had been one of the bravest and shrewdest of the Greek warriors in the Trojan War. The wooden horse that had brought down the city walls had been his idea. What if one of the wretched suitors found him sleeping on the beach? His throat would be slit before he could open his eyes. Surely he deserved better than that.

With a gesture of her hand the Goddess covered the island with a white, swirling mist. Then she strapped on her sandals of burnished gold, seized her spear and flashed down out of the sky until she was standing just a short distance from where Odysseus was lying.

The sun rose and shone through the white mist. The opaque light woke Odysseus. He sat up and rubbed his eyes. He looked about him. All he could see was mist.

'Where am I? What is this place? Where has my bitter destiny driven me to now?'

Then he saw, not far away, that there was the dim outline of a figure. Taking it for a shepherd or a fisherman, he said, 'Stranger, tell me, where am I? What is this place?'

Athene answered him with the voice of a man. 'You must be a fool or a dolt if you don't know this place! This place is famous from Troy to the Ocean Streams, from the rising to the setting of the sun — this is the island of Ithaca!'

Odysseus peered into the mist, and Athene walked towards him, her grey eyes shining with light.

She laughed. 'Noble Odysseus, you are home at last!'

She reached down and lifted the mist, as though she was lifting a curtain. Suddenly Odysseus saw Mount Neriton, he saw the beetling rocks, the hills, the terraced fields, the cliffs and the beaches of his native land — his own homeland. He threw himself down on to the ground and kissed the nourishing earth.

Athene shook his shoulder. 'Odysseus,' she said, 'there is no time to be wasted. First of all we must hide these great chests of treasure!'

She helped him lift the chests and carry them to a cave. She caused a huge stone to roll in front of the cave entrance.

'Odysseus,' she said, 'listen, the situation is this: you are home, but alone, unknown, under a strange sail and there is danger waiting where there should be a welcome.'

Athene told Odysseus about the suitors who had invaded his feasting hall. She told him about Penelope's long, lonely wait and the weaving and unravelling of her loom. She told him how Telemachus had made a great journey to Sparta, to visit red-haired Menelaus and beautiful Helen, in search of news of his father. And she told him that the suitors were planning to murder Telemachus on his return.

When she had finished speaking Odysseus drew his dagger from his belt. 'Goddess, if you would fight alongside me now, as you fought alongside us Greeks when we brought down Troy's shining diadem of towers, I swear the floors of my hall would soon run red with blood!'

But Athene lifted her shining fingers and touched his lips. 'Shh, Odysseus, I had thought you were becoming wise. This is no time for acts of daring folly.'

Odysseus shuddered at the sudden surge of bloodlust and a thousand blood-soaked memories that it carried in its wake. He pushed the dagger back into its scabbard.

Athene smiled fondly. 'Odysseus, you must go as an old man now.'

She touched Odysseus's shoulder with her hand. As she touched him his shoulders stooped, the hawk-like light went out of his eyes, his auburn curls whitened, his arms grew thin, his hands began to tremble, and he found that he was dressed in nothing but rags. 'You must go as an old beggar now. Do not return to your feasting hall but go rather to the hut of your faithful swineherd Eumaeus. Do not reveal yourself to him, but listen and you will learn much.'

Odysseus nodded, then he turned and hobbled up the hill with his back to the beach. Athene stood and watched him for a while, then she turned on her heel and swift as thought, she flashed across the sea to Sparta.

She made her way to the palace of red-haired Menelaus and beautiful Helen. She entered the bedchamber where Telemachus was lying fast asleep on a silver bed covered with purple blankets.

She coughed discreetly. Telemachus woke with the little hairs on the back of his neck prickling. He knew he was in the presence of one of the mighty Gods or Goddesses.

'Telemachus!'

He opened his eyes and gasped. Athene was standing shimmering beside his bed. 'Telemachus. The time has come for you to go home. Your mother Penelope has been discovered by the suitors, unravelling the shroud on her loom by moonlight. She has been forced to finish it. Now she must choose a new husband. You must go home, but be careful. The suitors are planning to murder you on your return. Do not go to your father's feasting hall. Go rather to the hut of your faithful swineherd Eumaeus.' Suddenly the Goddess was gone.

Telemachus was filled with spirit and awe. Straight away he prepared for his journey home.

10 ·FATHER·AND·SON·

Meanwhile, Odysseus, in the shape of an old beggar, was climbing the hill towards the hut of Eumaeus the swineherd. When Eumaeus saw the beggar he threw open the door of his hut.

'It has been decreed by mighty Zeus that anyone approaching one's threshold in peace should be welcomed. Old man, come inside, sit down.' The swineherd welcomed the beggar and showed him where he could sit. Then he slaughtered a fatted hog. When he had made sacrifices to the mighty Gods and Goddesses he roasted the meat over the flames of the fire. He gave the best cut to the beggar.

Gratefully the old beggar ate. Eumaeus settled down beside him and told him story after story about the outrages that had been committed by the suitors in Odysseus's feasting hall. As he listened, Odysseus felt the bile rising in his throat and his heart pounding against his ribs. But he bit his lip and swallowed and said nothing. When at last the swineherd fell silent, the old beggar turned to his host and said,

'In my travels from city to city and from port to port, I have heard rumours in many places that Odysseus is now on his way home, and that he sails with chests filled with treasure.'

Eumaeus shook his head.

'Old man, I can see you are trying to win your way into my heart with tittle-tattle and half-remembered gossip. No, Odysseus is dead. I feel it in my bones. His body is rolling somewhere deep beneath the blue waves of the sea.'

For three days Odysseus stayed with the swineherd. Every morning, when Eumaeus took his pigs to graze and root for truffles, he wandered the island. In the shape of an old beggar he climbed Mount Neriton. He wandered the vineyards, the terraced hills, the cliffs and the beaches. His heart sang for joy to feel Ithacan soil against the soles of his feet. He watched his people at work. He even watched his own father, old Laertes, harvesting grapes. No one took any notice of him. To them he was just another ragged old man who had had more than his share of bad luck. Sometimes out of pure pity someone would give him a cup of water or some bread and cheese.

It was on the morning of the fourth day that Telemachus returned. The swineherd was preparing breakfast. The old beggar was sitting on a stool by the fire. Suddenly the door swung open and standing framed in the doorway was a young man with his first beard on his chin. Eumaeus dropped the bowl he was holding.

'Telemachus! By the mighty Gods, you are safely home!' He ran across and threw his arms around the young man's neck. He kissed his forehead, his left eye, his right eye, his lips, his left hand, his right hand — the swineherd honoured his prince like a father honouring his son.

Odysseus, sitting on the stool by the fire, saw his son for the first time for nineteen years. He said nothing. He slowly got up to his feet and offered his stool. Telemachus shook his head.

'No, no, old man, you are a guest here. To me this is more of a second home. Sit down, sit down!'

The old beggar sat down again. Telemachus walked across and squatted in front of the fire, warming the palms of his hands. Eumaeus prepared breakfast for the three of them. They sat at the wooden table and ate. As they were eating Telemachus told them about his journey to

Sparta, about his encounter with red-haired Menelaus and beautiful Helen and about the visit he had received from the Goddess. When the food was finished he turned to Eumaeus. 'My mother, sweet Penelope, will have heard of these plans to murder me on my return. Her heart will be wrung with worry for me. Please, I beg you, go and tell her that I am safely home.'

The swineherd nodded and strapped on his sandals. He made his way across the floor of the hut and pushed open the door. It was at that moment that Odysseus saw Athene, her grey eyes blazing with light. Unseen by the swineherd she was standing outside the hut, beckoning urgently.

As soon as the swineherd was gone, the old beggar stood up and nodded to Telemachus. He hobbled through the door and closed it behind him. Athene whispered, 'Odysseus, the time has come for you to reveal yourself to your son.'

She reached forward and touched his shoulder with her hand. At once the light came back into his eyes, his thick

curls returned, his arms thickened. The beautiful cloak of King Alcinous hung over his broad shoulders. He turned and pushed open the door.

Telemachus got up to his feet in astonishment.

'Who are you? You are not the man you were before! Are you one of the mighty Gods who rule over the broad skies?'

Odysseus shook his head. 'Telemachus, I am no God. Look into my face and tell me, do you not see something of yourself?'

Telemachus came across and peered into the stranger's eyes. Suddenly his face lit up with joy.

'It's you! My father, you are home at last! When did you get here? How long have you been here? How did you get home?'

Odysseus's eyes filled with tears. 'Telemachus, my son!'

He reached and held his son in his arms. They sat down together in front of the fire and all that day Odysseus told Telemachus about his adventures on the fields of Troy and

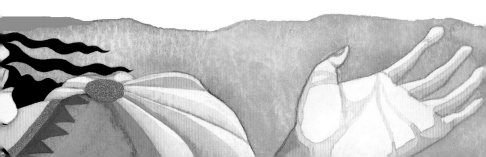

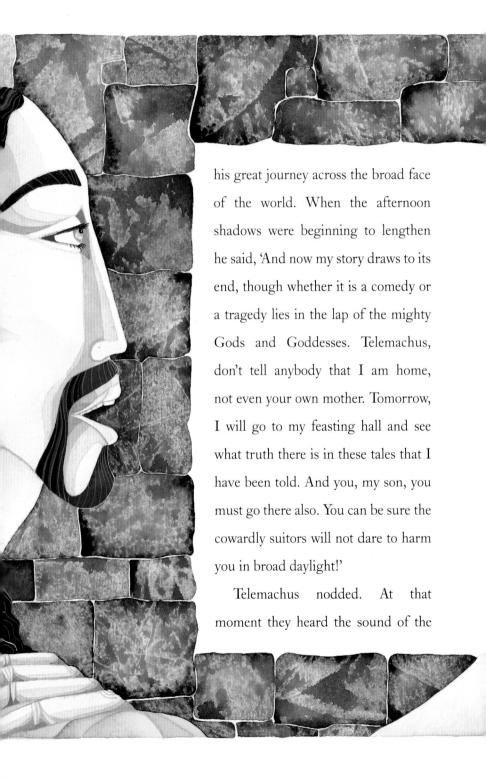

his great journey across the broad face of the world. When the afternoon shadows were beginning to lengthen he said, 'And now my story draws to its end, though whether it is a comedy or a tragedy lies in the lap of the mighty Gods and Goddesses. Telemachus, don't tell anybody that I am home, not even your own mother. Tomorrow, I will go to my feasting hall and see what truth there is in these tales that I have been told. And you, my son, you must go there also. You can be sure the cowardly suitors will not dare to harm you in broad daylight!'

Telemachus nodded. At that moment they heard the sound of the

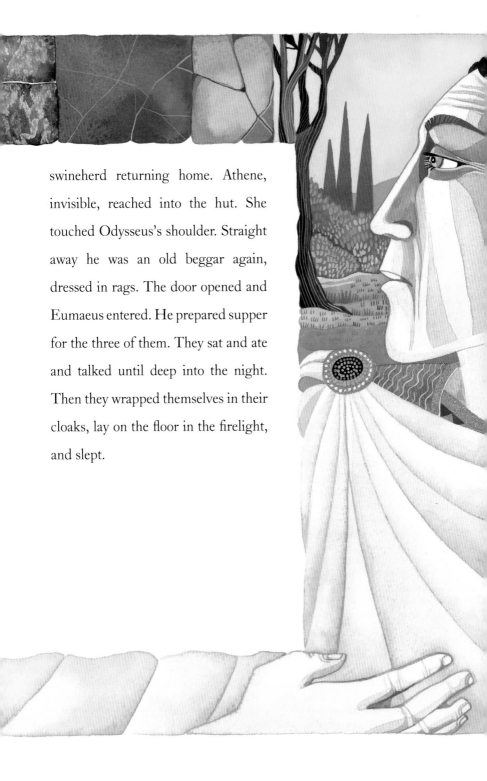

swineherd returning home. Athene, invisible, reached into the hut. She touched Odysseus's shoulder. Straight away he was an old beggar again, dressed in rags. The door opened and Eumaeus entered. He prepared supper for the three of them. They sat and ate and talked until deep into the night. Then they wrapped themselves in their cloaks, lay on the floor in the firelight, and slept.

11 ·THE·BEGGAR·

The next morning it was Telemachus who was the first to make the journey across the island and up the hill to the feasting hall. Already the suitors were enjoying themselves at Odysseus's expense: feasting, drinking, talking, laughing, singing. Telemachus came to the door. He stepped on to the threshold stone, lifted the latch and pushed the door open.

The suitors fell silent. They stared at him. Telemachus smiled grimly. 'Yes, it is me. I am home. Perhaps it was my corpse you were hoping to see, carried through these doors and laid out on one of the tables. Or maybe my ghost, my shade, walking through the closed doors. But no, it is me — skin, flesh, bone and beating heart.'

He made his way across the hall, threading between the tables and up the stairs to his mother's lonely bedchamber. When Penelope saw Telemachus she ran across and threw her arms around his neck. She soaked his shoulder with her tears. Telemachus told her about his journey to Sparta. He told her how he had met red-haired Menelaus and beautiful Helen. He told her how Menelaus had explained that Odysseus was being held captive by a nymph called Calypso on an island far, far, far across the blue waves of the sea. Penelope shook her head.

'If he was going to come home I feel sure he would have returned by now. And now the time has come for me to choose a new husband. But which one to choose? And how to choose him?'

Telemachus swallowed the urge to tell his mother the joyful news that Odysseus had indeed returned home.

Meanwhile Odysseus, in the shape of an old beggar, was crossing the island. He came to the hill and began to follow the winding path that led up to his hall. Everything was exactly as he remembered it, except for the sounds of rowdy feasting coming through the closed doors of the hall. As he climbed the hill he passed a dung heap. Lying

on top of it there was an ancient dog. When the old dog saw the beggar, it lifted its head and sniffed at the air. Its thin, leathery tail began to wag. It pulled itself up on to its spindly legs, hobbled across and licked the old beggar's hand. Odysseus looked down and he recognised Argos his faithful dog, whom he had trained as a puppy all those long years before.

But in the moment of the old dog's happiness death struck. Argos suddenly crumpled and fell lifeless on to the ground at his feet. Odysseus reached down and lifted the dog gently in his arms. He picked it up and laid it tenderly on the soft grass. As he looked down at the dead dog, he remembered the welcome he had once imagined for himself as he sailed away from the shores of Troy.

He wiped away a tear and carried on climbing the hill. He stepped on to the threshold stone. He lifted the latch

and pushed open the door of his hall. His ears were filled with the sounds of drunken laughter, and his nostrils with the smell of sweat and smoke, spilled wine and roasting meat. He entered and made his way from table to table, his arms outstretched, begging for food.

Not one of the suitors, not one of the revellers, took any notice of the old beggar until he came to the back of the hall. Sitting at a table covered with wooden dishes of sliced meat and half-empty wineskins was a suitor whose name was Antinous. When he saw the old beggar he shouted, 'Go away! Take your filthy, flea-bitten, moth-eaten carcass elsewhere before we throw you to the dogs!'

It was at that moment that Telemachus came down from his mother's bedchamber.

'Antinous,' he said, 'not only do you eat us out of house and home, you also break the sacred laws of hospitality in my father's feasting hall. Old man, come, sit down.'

With great kindness and consideration Telemachus showed the old beggar where he could sit. He fetched meat, bread and wine. He broke the bread with his own hands and gave it to the beggar.

Gratefully Odysseus ate and drank. When his plate was empty he got to his feet and went back to the table where Antinous was sitting. He stretched out his hands once more. 'Perhaps now you will think again, or do you begrudge an old beggar the crumbs from another man's table?' Antinous glared at him.

'I'll give you something. I'll give you something and no mistake!' He picked up a stool. He drew back his hand and with all the strength of his arm he hurled the stool at the old beggar. The stool struck Odysseus hard on the shoulder,

but he didn't falter or fall to the ground. He stood firm and the stool clattered on to the floor at his feet. The suitors watched the old beggar turn and walk across the feasting hall without saying a word. They watched as he sat down among the shadows by the door and brooded in silence. Then they shrugged and laughed and resumed their drunken feasting.

The story of the old beggar and the stool spread from the servants to maidservants. From the maidservants the story reached the ears of Penelope, upstairs in her lonely bedchamber.

That night she came quietly down the stairs. The suitors had either staggered drunkenly homewards or were sleeping with their cheeks in pools of spilled wine on the tabletops. Except for the occasional grunt or snore, everything in the hall was silent. The old beggar was still sitting among the shadows by the door. Penelope whispered, 'Old man, old man, come upstairs, I would like to speak with you.'

12 ·SETTING·THE·TRAP·

Odysseus looked up and saw his wife. He saw his wife for the first time in nineteen years. His heart soared for joy but he bit his lip, swallowed and said nothing. He got to his feet and followed her up the stairs to her bedchamber.

'Old man,' she said, 'old man, sit down. I would like to speak with you. I have heard about you from my faithful swineherd Eumaeus. He tells me that you have heard rumours that my husband, Odysseus, is on his way home, with chests filled with treasure.'

The old beggar shook his head. 'Rumours, madam, nothing but rumours.'

'I have heard nothing but rumours for nineteen long years,' Penelope said. 'Now the time has come for me to choose a new husband and bid farewell for ever to these walls that welcomed me as a wife all those years ago.'

The old beggar sighed. 'Madam, I can see your sorrows match my own. But tell me, which one of these wretched suitors will you choose? And how will you choose him?'

'Old man, I have been thinking about it all day and I have a plan. Years ago, before he went to fight in distant Troy, my husband's favourite sport was archery. Sweet Odysseus would take his bow, which still hangs from a wooden peg on the wall of the feasting hall, and he would draw a bowstring across it. Then twelve axes would be set in a row the length of the feasting hall: twelve ceremonial axes, one behind the other, with their blades to the ground, their handles pointing upwards, and the rings of their handles in a row. When everything had been made ready, Odysseus — I can see him now as though it was yesterday — would take an arrow and fit it to the bowstring. He would draw the bowstring back and loose the arrow through the rings of all twelve ceremonial axe handles. Nobody could match him.

'I will set the suitors the same task and whoever comes closest to Odysseus in skill I will take as a new husband.

'But, old man, it wasn't to pour my heart out to you that I invited you up here this evening. I have had a dream and often you travelling people are skilled at reading such things.'

'Then, madam, tell me your dream,' the old beggar said to Penelope.

'In my dream I kept a flock of fat white geese. I kept them in my husband's hall and every day I fed them with my own hands. Then, in my dream, an eagle swooped down from the mountains, flew through the door of the hall, slaughtered all the fat white geese, then sat on a rafter and sang.'

The old beggar chuckled. 'Madam, that dream is easily understood. The geese are the suitors who feast in your husband's hall. The eagle is Odysseus and one day he will return and kill all of them!'

'Yes, yes, yes, old man, I know that. But dreams come to us through two gates: either through a gate of ivory or through a gate of horn. Those dreams that come to us through the curved and decorated gate of ivory are mere fancies, fantasies. But the dreams that come to us through the burnished gate of horn carry the truth. Which gate did my dream come through, old man?'

The old beggar looked at the floor between his feet. 'I wish I knew,' he said, 'I wish I knew.'

Penelope sighed, 'So do I.' Then she turned and called over her shoulder, 'Eurycleia, Eurycleia!' The door opened and an ancient servant hobbled into the room. Odysseus recognised her instantly. Eurycleia had been his nursemaid. She had suckled him when he was a baby and looked after him when he was a child.

'Eurycleia,' Penelope said, 'take this old beggar, wash his feet, and give him a new warm woollen cloak for his old shoulders.'

The old woman beckoned to Odysseus. 'Old man, come with me, come with me.' The beggar got up to his feet and followed her.

She led the beggar out of the bedchamber and she showed him a bench where he could sit. She fetched a bowl of steaming water. She took off his sandals and she washed his feet. She washed his ankles. She washed his calves. She washed his knees. Then suddenly the old woman stopped. She stared in astonishment. Up the inside of the old beggar's thigh she had seen a scar, a jagged scar. She'd

recognised it instantly as a scar that Odysseus had received from the tusk of a wild boar when he was a boy. She looked up into the old beggar's face.

'It's you! You are home at last!'

The old beggar reached down and pressed his hand over her mouth. 'Shh, woman! If you love me, hold your tongue! Say nothing!' The old nursemaid nodded, her wrinkled face beaming with delight. She hobbled off, fetched a warm woollen cloak, and gave it to the old beggar. He threw it over his shoulder and he winked at Eurycleia. She smiled fondly back at him.

Odysseus made his way downstairs to the dark, silent feasting hall. He saw Telemachus sitting alone. He whispered, 'My son, come here. Listen to me and do exactly what I tell you. Take all the weapons that are hanging from the walls and hide them in a locked chamber. If anybody asks you where they are, tell them they've become tarnished and smoke-blackened and they've gone to be cleaned and sharpened. Leave only my own bow hanging from its wooden peg and the twelve ceremonial axes. Then, when everything is ready, hide a bow for yourself among the shadows by the door and also hide two quivers full of arrows, two swords and two bronze-tipped spears. Then go to old Eurycleia. She alone has recognised me and knows my secret. Tell her that tomorrow, when I signal to her, she is to make her way out of the feasting hall and she is to lock all the doors from the outside.'

Straight away Telemachus set to work.

Odysseus went outside. He lay down on some soft grass under the countless stars. He wrapped himself in his warm woollen cloak, whispered a prayer to owl-eyed Athene, closed his eyes and fell into the sweet oblivious balm of sleep.

13 ·SPRINGING·THE·TRAP·

Odysseus was woken by the sun shining on to his face. Already the suitors were gathered, feasting and drinking. He got up to his feet and made his way to the hall. He stepped on to the threshold stone, lifted the latch and pushed the door open. He went from table to table, his arms outstretched, begging for food.

One of the suitors said, 'Look, the old beggar is back!'

'Old man, come here,' said another, 'have some wine!' He offered a cup of wine. The beggar walked over, but as he reached to take it, the suitor drew back his hand and tipped the wine over the old man's head.

'Old man, have a piece of meat!' said another suitor. He picked up the shinbone of an ox and hurled it at the beggar, striking him on the forehead so that the red blood trickled down with the red wine. All the suitors threw back their heads and bellowed with laughter. But then, suddenly, their laughter stopped. Penelope was coming down the stairs from her bedchamber. She was dressed in bright silks, with

her hair hanging loose over her shoulders. Old Eurycleia was hobbling down behind her. When Penelope reached the bottom of the stairs, she stopped and turned to the suitors.

'For years you have fastened on my husband's hall as your place of perpetual feasting. Your excuse has always been that you want to win my hand in marriage, and now the time has come for me to put you to the test.'

She reached across and took the bow from its wooden peg on the wall.

'Whoever comes closest to matching my husband in skill, whoever can draw a string across this bow and loose an arrow through the rings of twelve ceremonial axe handles, he will be the one that I take as a new husband. The time has come for me to bid farewell for ever to these walls that welcomed me as a wife all those years ago.'

Penelope turned and nodded to Eurycleia. Straight away the old woman set to work. She took the twelve axes from the wall. She set them one behind the other, the blades to the ground, the handles pointing upwards, the rings in a

row, just as she remembered Odysseus doing it all those
years before.

When everything was ready, Penelope turned to the
suitors again. 'Now, which one of you is man enough to
win me?'

There was a great hubbub and discussion among the
suitors then as to who should go first. They decided to take
turns, following the direction that the wine jug took when
it was passed from hand to hand. The first to try was called
Leodes. He took the bow in his fat white hand, swollen from
months of feasting. He set the foot of the bow on the floor at
his feet. He began to try to bend it. It sprang out of his hand
and clattered down on to the ground. A second suitor tried
and fared no better. Each of them in turn tried to string the
bow and not one of them could do it. Some came closer than
others, but not one of them succeeded. So they warmed the
bow in front of the fire and they rubbed beeswax into the
wood to make it more supple. Each of them tried again and
still not one of them could string the bow.

Penelope stood with her arms folded and she watched. She shook her head. 'Perhaps the day is not a lucky one,' she said. 'Perhaps the day is not auspicious.'

She turned and made her way back up the stairs. Eurycleia followed, hobbling up slowly behind.

As the old nursemaid climbed the stairs, the beggar, sitting among the shadows by the door, caught her eye. He winked and nodded. Eurycleia smiled. As soon as she was out of sight she made her way out of the hall by a back way. She hurried round to the threshold stone, and she pulled the bolts across the doors, locking them firmly from the outside.

Inside the hall there was silence, broken at last by Antinous. 'It's not so much losing the woman I mind. She's pretty enough, I grant you, but there are plenty of other fish in the sea. No! It's making ourselves seem such weaklings beside the memory of that cursed Odysseus!'

The other suitors nodded and spat on the ground. Then a voice came echoing from the shadows by the door. 'I was an archer once, in the days of my youth.'

Antinous turned and looked at the old beggar. He lifted his lip in a sneering smile. 'You might have been an archer once, but now you are nobody!'

The beggar continued, 'I was an archer in the days of my youth, and I wonder if there is still strength enough in these old, weather-beaten arms to draw a string across that bow.'

The suitors threw back their heads and laughed. A hail of bones and broken crockery flew across the feasting hall, but then Telemachus got up to his feet and raised his hand.

'Enough!' he said. 'Enough! Antinous, are you afraid that this old beggar will put you to shame?' He smiled at the beggar. 'Old man, show us what you can do!' He gave the bow to the old beggar. Odysseus felt the smooth familiar wood against his hands for the first time in nineteen years.

He set the foot of the bow on to the floor at his feet. Slowly, taking his time, he began to bend it. Slowly he drew the string across it. And then with one finger, as though he was playing the string of a lyre, he plucked the bowstring. It gave a beautiful clear note, like a swallow's song.

From high above the roof of the feasting hall there came an answering rumble of thunder. The suitors sat and they stared. Then the old beggar took an arrow and he fitted it to the bowstring.

He drew the bowstring back and loosed the arrow. It flew clean through the rings of the twelve ceremonial axe handles and lodged quivering in the wall beyond.

The suitors gaped google-eyed.

The old beggar smiled. 'That match is played and won! Now for the second!' He took another arrow, fitted it to the bowstring, drew the bowstring back and loosed the arrow. It flew straight through the throat of Antinous. He fell face down on the ground, his legs kicking. And then he was dead.

The suitors leaped to their feet.

The old beggar jumped up on to a table and Telemachus jumped up beside him. Athene, invisible, reached into the hall.

She touched the old beggar's shoulder. Straight away the hawk-like light came back to the eyes. The broad shoulders, the thick arms, the fine clothes and the dark curls returned. The suitors ran to the walls to grab weapons — but all the weapons were gone.

Odysseus and Telemachus loosed arrow after arrow after arrow. The suitors ran to the doors. They rattled

and shook them — but they were locked from the outside.

Again and again, father and son loosed their arrows. When all the arrows were spent each made his way across the hall, with a sword in one hand and a spear in the other, swinging and slicing like reapers in a field, gathering a grim harvest of death.

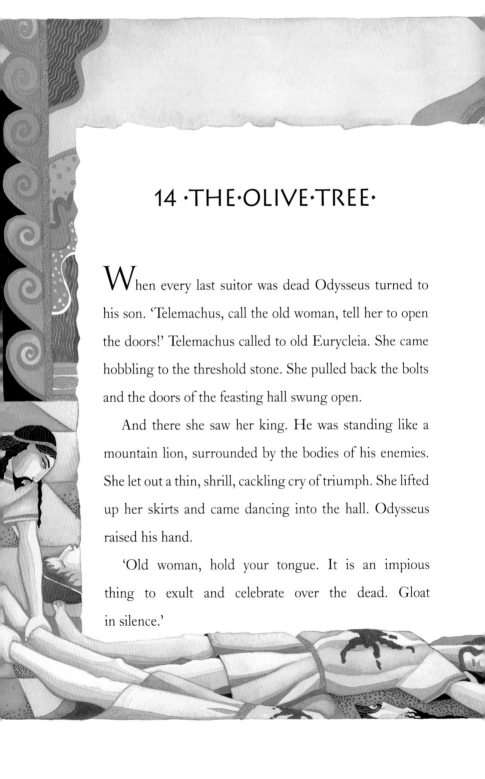

14 ·THE·OLIVE·TREE·

When every last suitor was dead Odysseus turned to his son. 'Telemachus, call the old woman, tell her to open the doors!' Telemachus called to old Eurycleia. She came hobbling to the threshold stone. She pulled back the bolts and the doors of the feasting hall swung open.

And there she saw her king. He was standing like a mountain lion, surrounded by the bodies of his enemies. She let out a thin, shrill, cackling cry of triumph. She lifted up her skirts and came dancing into the hall. Odysseus raised his hand.

'Old woman, hold your tongue. It is an impious thing to exult and celebrate over the dead. Gloat in silence.'

Eurycleia stood still and lowered her head. 'Old woman,' Odysseus continued, 'fetch servants and maidservants with buckets, sponges and water. Clean every speck of blood from this feasting hall. Telemachus, you and I will burn the bodies of the dead!'

Odysseus and Telemachus grabbed the corpses of the suitors by their ankles, dragged them across the hall and down the hill. They built a huge pyre and lit the funeral fire. All that day the heat of the fire's heart consumed the houses of bone. When all had been reduced to smouldering white ash, Odysseus and Telemachus climbed back up the hill. They entered the hall. It was spotless. There was no trace or fleck or speck of blood.

Odysseus called Eurycleia. 'Old woman,' he said, 'go upstairs and tell my wife Penelope that her husband is home and he is waiting for her!'

Eurycleia nodded. She lifted her skirts and twinkled up the stairs to the bedchamber as though

she had forgotten all her years. Penelope was lying fast asleep on her bed. All day she had been sleeping, her heart heavy with sorrow. The old woman said, 'Madam! Madam! Wake up, wake up, wake up!'

Penelope sat up and rubbed her eyes.

'Madam, wake up. Your husband is home! He is downstairs! He is waiting for you!'

Penelope looked at Eurycleia and shook her head. 'Old woman, what are you talking about? Has one of the mighty Gods or Goddesses addled your wits?'

Eurycleia wrung her hands. 'For pity's sake, madam, come downstairs!'

Penelope climbed out of bed. She followed the old woman down the stairs. She saw there was a man standing in the feasting hall. She stood on the bottom step. She looked at him and she said nothing.

Telemachus said, 'Mother, strange cold-hearted mother, your husband is home after nineteen years and you stand there and you say nothing?'

Odysseus turned to Telemachus. 'Leave us alone.' He turned to his servants and his maidservants who were lined up along the walls watching. 'Leave us alone now.'

As soon as the last one had left the room, Penelope walked across the hall. She looked into his face and said, 'Is it you? You are so changed!' She reached and touched his cheek with her fingertips. 'I do not know you any longer. I do not even know that it is you. You are not the young man I remember sailing off to fight in distant Troy all those years ago, leaving me standing on the seashore with a baby in my arms.'

She turned away from him. 'I cannot sleep with you. I will not share a bed with you. I will tell the servants to move the bed. You can sleep on the other side of a closed door.'

Odysseus put his hand tenderly on her shoulder and whispered, 'Penelope, you know that cannot be. You know that I built this hall around an ancient olive tree. You know that I carved our bed with my own hands from one of the branches of that tree. You know that there is no one who can lift it and set it on the other side of a closed door.'

Suddenly Penelope turned, her eyes shining with delight. She seized his hands.

'Then it is you! Then it is you!' she cried. 'Nobody knows the secret of our bed — you and I alone!'

Odysseus looked into her face. She looked into his. Tears of joy were streaming down their cheeks. Suddenly she was in his arms. 'Penelope,' he said. 'Penelope, my wife, my queen, only now am I truly home.'

That night Odysseus, Penelope and Telemachus sat down together in the feasting hall. With them was Odysseus's old father Laertes, the faithful swineherd Eumaeus, and old Eurycleia. Odysseus listened as each of them told the story of all that had happened on the island of Ithaca during his long absence. There were tears at the death of his mother and there was laughter at Penelope's trick with the loom.

There was anger at the outrages of the suitors and gratitude at the interventions of owl-eyed Athene. When the stories had been told, Odysseus refilled his cup with wine and told of his adventures on the fields of Troy and his great journey across the broad face of the world. And then he filled his cup again and told of the one adventure still left to make — that journey far inland to the place where the oar he was carrying over his shoulder would be mistaken for a winnowing fan.

But Penelope put her arm over his shoulder and silenced his mouth with her kisses. 'Sweet Odysseus,' she said, 'that will be as it may be and as the mighty Gods decree. But now you are here, in my arms, at home, in the place where all past and all future melt into present joy.'

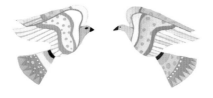

Dreams and visions come through two gates: either through a gate of ivory or through a gate of horn. If the dream, the vision, comes through the ivory gate, it is mere fancy, fantasy. If it comes through the gate of horn it carries truth. This dream, this vision, is over. You must decide through which gate it has come.